# MORT

By Morgan Swank

Illustrated by Daniel Hills

Printed in the United States of America.

*For my mama vulture, who always came flying after me when I needed her. For Eve, also. May kindness be your flock.*

Mort the baby vulture sits in his tree watching the
antelope graze nearby.
He licks his beak because he hasn't eaten all day.

"Mama? Are you here? I'm hungry!" Mort calls.
He jumps out of the tree and falls to the ground with a thud, causing an antelope stampede.

Mort hides under a rock. Kinglsey the kingfisher swoops down to Mort. He is joined by his friends Valerie the lovebird and Melvin the mallard.

“Way to go bird brain.” Melvin snickers.
“Mort isn’t a bird, Melvin. He’s a Monster!” adds Kinsley.

"I am too a bird." says Mort. "Look at my wings!"
Mort lifts his wings, which makes him look big and scary.

"Yes, you have feathers, but what about your bald head and scary black eyes?" spits Kingsley. "Mort, you're just a bloody beak freak that would eat us if you got too hungry."

"That's not true!" Mort yells.
"That's not very nice." says Valerie. "Mort, you're a bird just like all of us.
You're just a little...different...and that's okay!
My beak is small, and Kingsley's feathers are blue. Sometimes we are different." Valerie chirps.

"Yeah, but none of us are weirdo boogey monsters." Melvin quacks.

“I’ll prove it! I’ll go live with the macaws in the jungles.” says Mort.
“I’ll show you all!”

Mort flies away in a hurry wiping off his tears, squeaking and sniffling into his little beak.

“Way to go bird brains.” Valerie says to Kingsley and Melvin before chasing after Mort.

Mort flies over the African savanna until he can't anymore.

"I'm so hungry and it is so hot. I have to find food."
cries Mort.
He sees some bones and feathers on the ground.
"No, I can't eat this. This isn't what real birds eat," his stomach grumbles, "but berries are!"

He eats some bright red berries from a nearby prickly bush and scrunches up his face.
"Blech!" says Mort. "These berries are sour!"

"I know what I'll do!" Mort says gleefully.
"I'll give myself more feathers. Then Kingsley will see I'm a real bird."

Mort breaks the bright red berries in his beak and covers his bald, white head in the sticky juice.
He pulls the feathers and leaves from the animal bones and glues them on his little body.

Hopping over to the watering hole, he takes a look.
"I'm a real bird!" he cries happily.

Valerie the lovebird watches from behind a rock nearby.
"Oh, Mort." sighs Valerie.

"I know who can help," she gasps, "Mort's mom! She'll know what to do."

Valerie flies away, flapping her tiny wings with all her might.

Valerie returns to her home and flies to the scary vulture tree.
Afraid she might become a snack, she tip-toes around quietly.
She sees Mort's mom, Carrion, is in her nest.
She is picking her teeth with a wishbone.

"Miss Carrion! Miss Carrion!"
"What is it, Valerie?" Carrion coos.
"Mort has gone to the edge of the savanna!"
"Why has he done that?" Carrion asks worriedly.
"The other birds made fun of him and called him Bloody Beak.
They said he wasn't a real bird. He ran away to prove he could live in the jungle with the other different birds."
"Why are they so mean to Mort?" Carrion asks.
"I think they're afraid of him and all of you because you're different, but I told Mort it doesn't mean he isn't just like one of us." Valerie cries.

The other vultures circle Valerie.

"Mort?" one asks.
"Mort's run away?" asks another.
"We have to go and find him!"

"Valerie, can you lead us to him?" Carrion asks.
"I think so," says Valerie, "but it will take a long time."

"Who will hunt the feast if we're gone?"
asks another vulture.
"We will have to let the hyenas take over." says Carrion.
"Now, come on. Let's find my baby."

Back on the edge of the savanna, Mort is trying to fly but is too weak and sick from the bad berries.
"Oh no!" says Mort. "How will I ever get back home? I'll have to stay here forever."

Mort plops down by the watering hole to take a sip and looks at his reflection.
Suddenly, a baby hippo pops out of the water.

"AGH!" Mort screams.
"Oh! Excuse me." says the hippo. "My name is Kubwa.
Who...and what are you?"
"My name is Mort. I'm a vul— I'm a bird."
"You look like a scary ghost." says Kubwa.

“No, I have feathers on my head and I have big, beautiful wings. See?”

Mort does a silly dance and a little bit of his feathers and berry juice falls off.
“Uhh, you’re shedding, Mort.” says Kubwa.
“Oh no!” Now they’ll never think I’m a real bird.”
sighs Mort.
“Who won’t?” Kubwa asks.
“The other birds back home. They’re so different than me and my family. They are afraid of me. I just wanted to fit in and now I’m not strong enough to get back home. I’m so hungry.”

Mort begins to cry.
“Don’t cry Mort.” Kubwa bumps noses to Morts beak.
“Everyone thinks I’m a scary, meanie water elephant until they get to know me.”

"What do you mean?" Mort sniffles.
"I eat the same things as you.
Sometimes I eat delicious grass, but without me a lot of other animals would die."

"Wow." says Mort. "You do sound important."

“I am! I help the fish get the food they need and the bring nutrients to the water we drink.”
says Kubwa.

“But vultures aren’t special.
We don’t help the fish or the animals like hippos."
says Mort.

"You are important too, Mort." says Kubwa.
"Just because you're different, doesn't mean you aren't special."

"Really?" Mort asks.

"Yes! You keep our home free of diseases and no other bird can do that. You make sure your friends don't get very sick every day. You are the only you and you are best Mort you can be."

"I never thought of it that way." Mort says.
"You need to get home to the other vultures and grow big and strong. It's not safe out here for a baby alone without a flock." says Kubwa.
"I'm too weak to make it home alone. I miss my mom and my vulture family!" Mort cries.

Over the horizon, a kettle of vultures comes flocking down toward the watering hole with Valerie the lovebird leading the way.

"Mama!" Mort yells.
"Oh, Mort! What were you thinking? And what are you wearing?" Carrion asks.
"I'm sorry mama. I wanted to be a real bird."
"Mort, you are a real bird."

Carrion takes water from the pond and washes the berry juice and feathers off Mort.
"You're a very special bird. Now, come on I'm taking you home."

"How did you know I was here?" asks Mort.
"I'm sorry, Mort." says Valerie
"I followed you and brought your mom here. I was worried about you."
"That's okay." says Mort. "Thanks for saving me. You're a good friend, Valerie.
Let's go home. Seeya Kubwa!"

Kubwa snorts water out of his snout.

Mort hops on his mother's back to ride off into the sunset with his family.

Back home on the reservation, the vultures see a pack of hyenas chasing
Kingsley the kingfisher and some magpies in a circle around their feast.

"Live food is always better." snarls the hyena.
"Come here little birdie." laughs another.
"I want the drumstick!" says another.
"We have to help them!" says Mort.

The vultures swoop towards the hyenas to drive them away.

Carrion drops Mort safely on the ground.
He puffs up his chest and squawks loudly.
"These are my friends and you're going to leave them alone!"

Carrion starts swooping and pecking at the last hyena before he yelps and runs away.

“Wow, thanks Mort.” Kingsley says sheepishly. “That was really brave of you.”
“Us birds have to look out for each other.” says Mort.

“Yeah I guess we do.” says Kingsley sheepishly.
“I’m sorry about all the mean stuff I said to you.
You’re a pretty cool bird,” Kingsley adds, “and you’re much better than the hyenas.”
“Thanks Kingsley. Friends?” asks Mort.
“Friends.”
Mort and Kingsley shake wings.

Mort hears his mom calling for him.

"Mort! You need to eat dinner and the hyenas left a large gazelle.
Come home!" yells Mort's mom.

"I have to go." says Mort.
"Sounds...delicious?" says Valerie.
"You can come over for dinner if you want?
All of you!" Mort says to his friends.

"No thank you. I'm, uhh, flying south for the winter." says Melvin the mallard.
"I just ate a gross dead gazelle yesterday actually." lies Kingsley the kingfisher.
"Thank you, Mort. That's very sweet of you," says Valerie the lovebird, "but I'll stick to fruit for now. Maybe we can play tomorrow?"
"Yes! Mort you want to join us?" Kingsley asks.
"If you want me to?" questions Mort.

"We'll see you tomorrow, Bloody Beak." Kinsley laughs.

Mort waves goodbye to his new friends and joins his mother, who wraps her big mom wings around him
lovingly as he gathers around the rest of his vulture family happily for a large dinner.

Made in the USA
Coppell, TX
25 January 2020

14982874R00038